for *Catherine*

First Chronicle Books LLC edition published in 2009.

Book design by Paul Rand.
Typeset in BodoniClassic.
Manufactured in China.

Library of Congress Cataloging-in-Publication Data
Rand, Ann.
I know a lot of things / by Ann & Paul Rand. — 1st Chronicle Books ed.
p. cm.
Summary: Celebrates the many things young children know about their world,
while looking forward to a time when they will know more.
ISBN 978-0-8118-6615-6
[1. Growth—Fiction.] I. Rand, Paul, 1914–1996. II. Title.
PZ7.R152Ik 2009
[E]—dc22
2008020680

10 9 8 7 6 5 4 3 2 1

Chronicle Books LLC
680 Second Street, San Francisco, California 94107

www.chroniclekids.com

I know
a lot
of
things

by Ann & Paul Rand

chronicle books·san francisco

I know such a lot of things . . .
I know when I look
in a mirror
what I see is me.

I know a cat goes meow

a dog goes bowwow
and that is how
they talk.

Of course I know
a horse can pull
a wagon full
of wood.

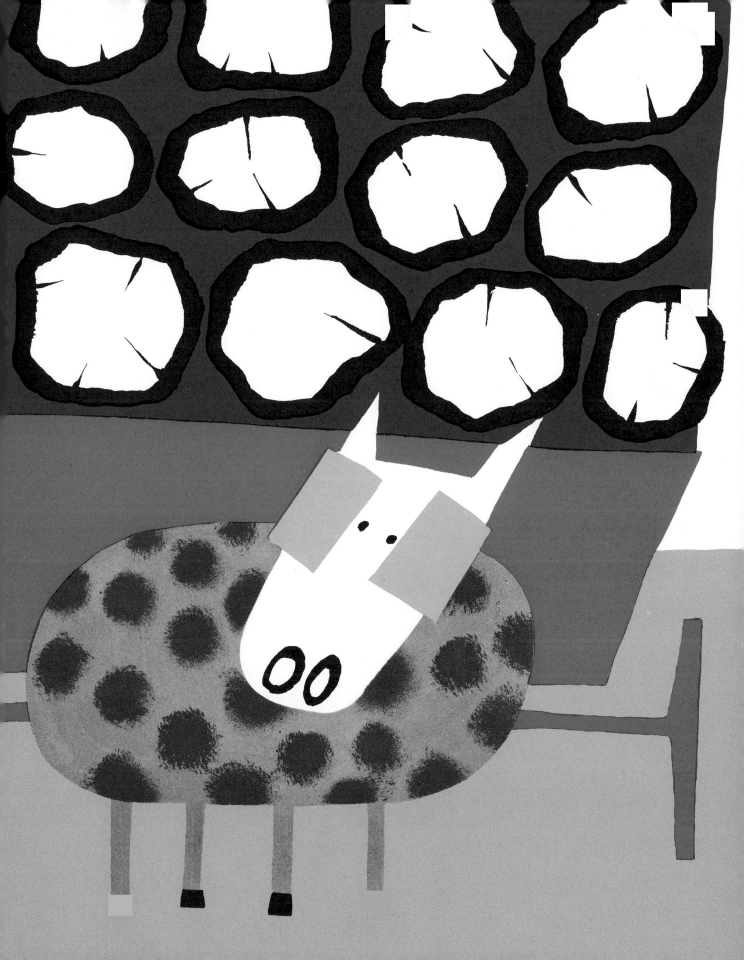

And even an ant
could carry
a load on his back
big as a berry

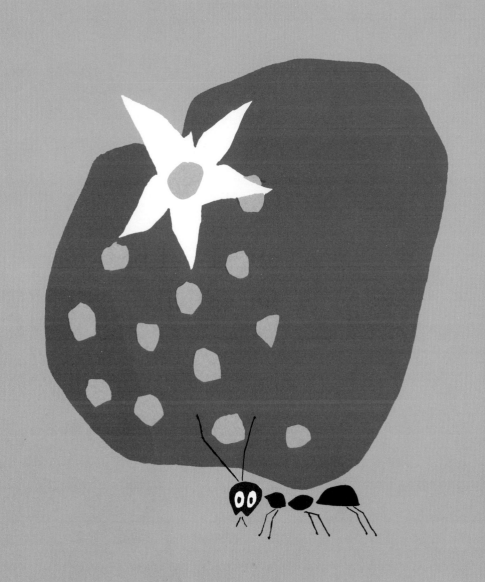

and a leaf be a ferry
for a snail.

I know that I can
hide
in a
cozy
cave

or ride a big blue wave

across the sea.

I know I can dig

a hole this big

and climb a tree
high as the sky
to watch a bird fly by
and an acorn drop
kerplop kerplop

or wave hello   to a mushroom

who's just a little fellow with a big umbrella.

I know how things are made.
A house has glass
and bricks
and lots of sticks.
A square box has
a top as wide
as its side.

A book needs pages
and a cake
takes
ages
to bake.

I know the world is wide,
and a star
is far away,
and the moon is a light
for the night,
and the sun
is round as a bun
and very bright.

Oh

I know

such

a

lot

of

things,

but

as

I

grow

I know

I'll

know

much

more.